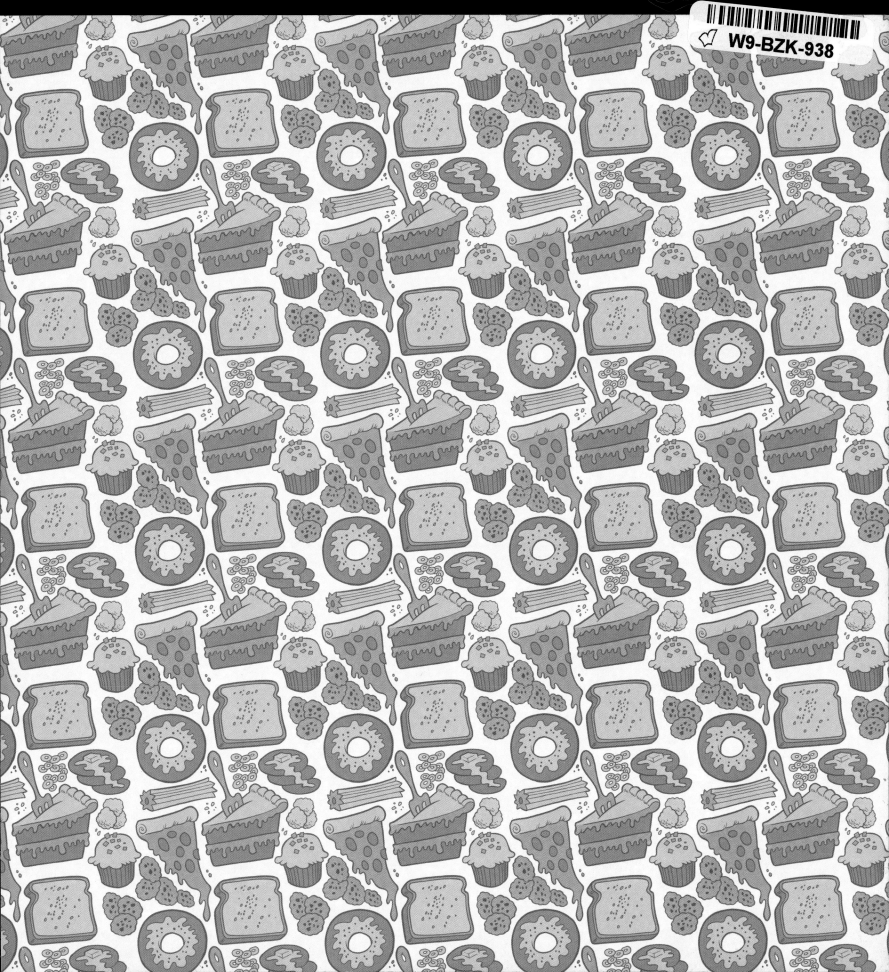

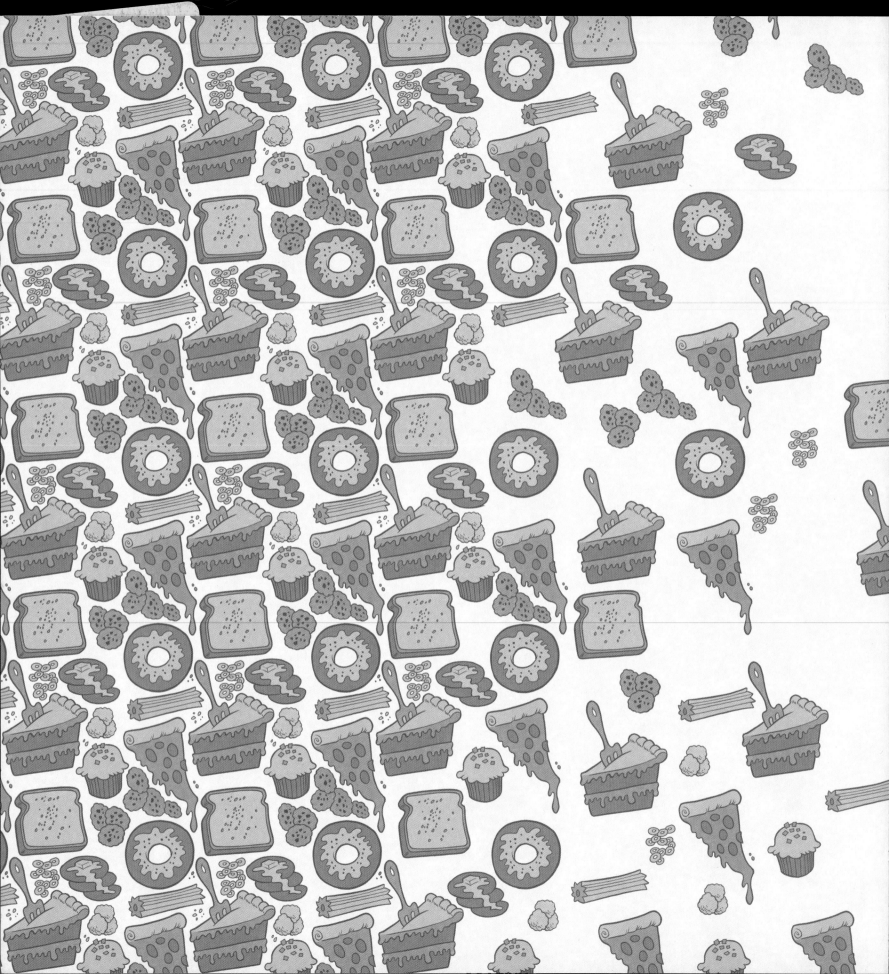

the GLUTEN GLITCH

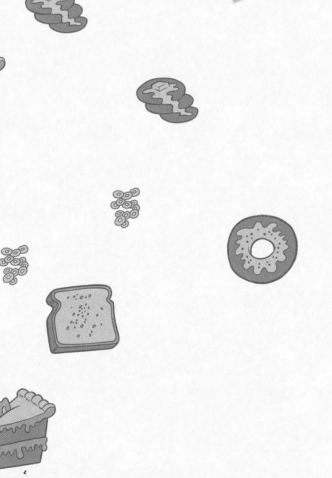

ISBN 13: 978-1-59298-467-1

Library of Congress Catalog Number: 2012904103
Printed in the United States of America
First Printing: 2012

16 15 14 13 12   5 4 3 2 1

Cover and interior design by Kevin Cannon

![Beaver's Pond Press logo] BEAVER'S POND
PRESS

Beaver's Pond Press, Inc.
7108 Ohms Lane
Edina, MN 55439-2129
(952) 829-8818
www.BeaversPondPress.com

To order, visit
www.BeaversPondBooks.com
or call 1-800-901-3480.

Reseller discounts
available.

This book is dedicated to my little food allergy warriors,
Ryan and Vance, who eat differently every day.

The information in this story shows what gluten *could* do to the body.
However, every child is different and the reaction will be as well. This book touches
on the emotional and social effect of eating gluten-free, and is not meant to be used
as a medical or health guide. Although gluten intolerance and celiac disease are
different conditions, this book can be comforting to all children who are on a gluten-
free diet and who always have to eat differently.

A portion of the profits from this book will go to FAAN (the Food
Allergy & Anaphylaxis Network) and the Celiac Disease Foundation.

"It's not fair!" sobbed Gideon as he climbed into the car.

He had not been allowed to have one of the cupcakes at the school party. And even though his mother gave him one of his safe cupcakes, his friends got to have ones that looked like farm animals.

"I'm sad, Mommy," cried Gideon. "I want the treats that the other kids get. Why can't I have them?"

"Another problem with gluten again, huh?" asked Mommy. "I'm sorry that you're upset."

"I hate eating gluten-free," grumbled Gideon.

"I know," said Mommy. "It's a real gluten glitch.

You want the same treats as your friends, but you can't
eat them, Gideon, because gluten makes you sick.
I think that we should talk about why you feel so bad."

The rest of the car ride home, Gideon and Mommy talked about why he shouldn't eat foods with gluten, and talking about it made Gideon feel better.

"Mommy, can you tell me the story again about why I can't eat gluten?" asked Gideon.

"When you were a baby," said Mommy, "you were fussy and had rashes all the time.

"We took you to the doctor and we found out that your body does not like gluten, and gluten was making you sick.

"We stopped feeding you foods with gluten, and guess what! You became one happy baby!"

"But I still want the cupcakes that the other kids got to have!" cried Gideon.

"I know that you want to eat cookies and cakes like your friends, or the ones that you see at the store. But those foods are made with wheat flour. Wheat flour has gluten in it," said Mommy.

"Why do my friends get to eat those things?" replied Gideon.

"Most people can eat gluten foods and
feel just fine," Mommy explained.

"But some people can't have gluten, just like you.
They cannot eat regular breads, muffins, cookies, or
crackers because gluten makes them very sick."

"Do you remember what happens when you eat gluten?" asked Mommy.

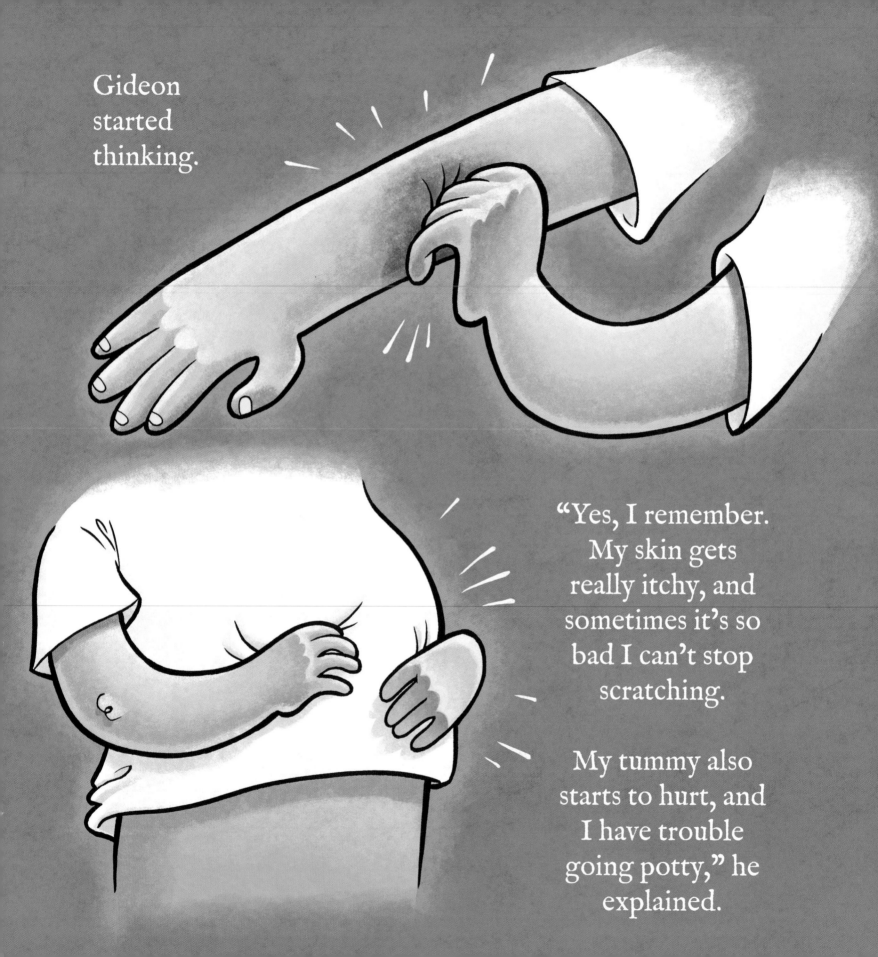

Gideon started thinking.

"Yes, I remember. My skin gets really itchy, and sometimes it's so bad I can't stop scratching.

My tummy also starts to hurt, and I have trouble going potty," he explained.

"Yes, that's all because of the gluten glitch!
Can you remember anything else that gluten does to
your body?" asked Mommy.

"Oh, I know!" Gideon said. "Gluten gives me a
headache, and sometimes it's hard for me to think."

"Very good, Gideon. Those are all reasons
why it's so important for you not to eat foods
with gluten in them," explained Mommy.

"I'll be able to eat regular cake on my next birthday, right Mommy?" asked Gideon.

Mommy looked at Gideon in the rearview mirror and gave him a sweet smile.

"Probably not," she said. "You might be able to eat gluten when you're older, or you might not. Some people can't eat gluten their whole lives. That is why you only eat safe foods. Daddy and I can make foods without gluten for you, or we can buy these foods at the store," she reminded him.

"Gideon, do you remember
how to tell if food is safe
to eat?" asked Mommy.

"Yes, I must always ask
if there is gluten in it,"
answered Gideon.

"But the other treats
just look so good!"

Gideon leaned back in his seat with his arms crossed. "It's still not fair," he said in a huff.

Mommy could tell that Gideon was still upset, and she wanted to cheer him up.

"There are many yummy treats that you can eat," said Mommy. "Let's play the *I Can Eat* game! We can each take turns naming treats that you can eat. I'll go first!"

"You can eat popsicles,"
said Mommy.

"I can eat vanilla ice cream,"
said Gideon.

"And you can eat cotton candy."

"I can eat fruit gummies,"
replied Gideon with a smile.

"And you can eat lollipops."

"And I can eat toasted marshmallows!"
Gideon said with a loud giggle.

"You bet, Gideon! And you can have a plain milk
chocolate bar to go with that!" said Mommy.

"I can also eat popcorn, potato chips, and corn
chip nachos!" Gideon called out from the back seat.

By now Gideon was laughing.
He thought about the delicious grape
fruit rolls he liked to tear off with his teeth.

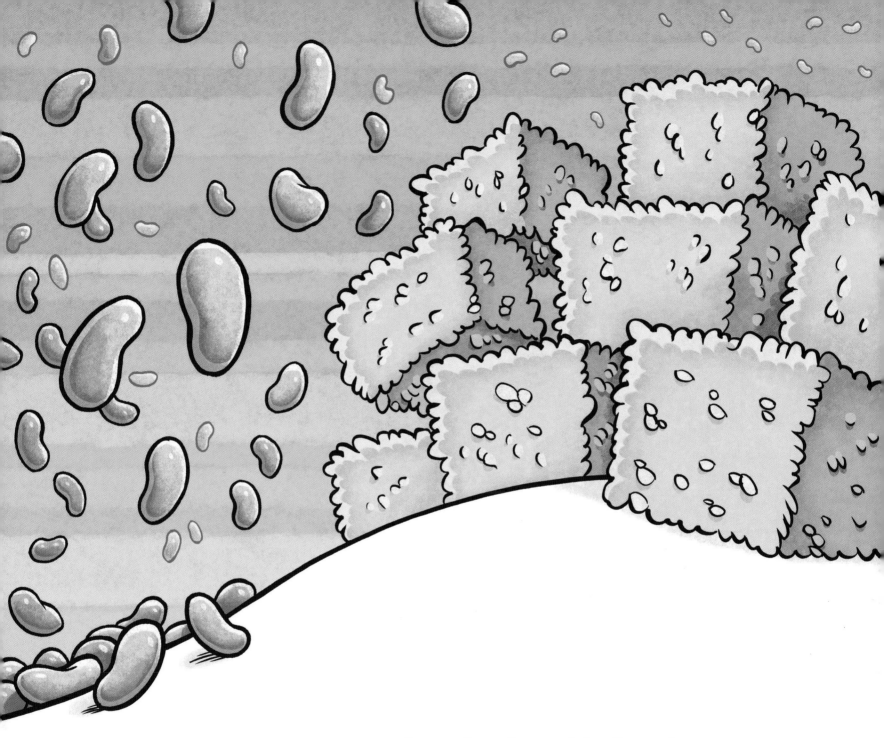

He thought about his favorite treat,
blueberry jellybeans, and he couldn't
forget the rice-trixie treats his mommy made.

Boy! Gideon was really getting hungry and he was feeling better about eating gluten-free.

"Mommy, can I have some ice cream when we get home?" asked Gideon.

"You certainly can," said Mommy, "as soon as you finish all of your dinner. It's TACO NIGHT!"

"Yeah, that's my favorite! No more gluten glitches today!" Gideon hollered as they pulled into their driveway.

TACO NIGHT!

One of the best dinners in the world for a gluten-free family is TACO NIGHT. Having a meal that everyone can share is an important aspect of living gluten-free for our family, as I'm sure it is for yours.

Here's to happy and healthy gluten-free living!

From my family to yours,

Stasie John

YOU WILL NEED:

½ cup chopped red or green bell pepper

celery seed

1 ½ lbs ground beef

2 cups cooked white or brown rice

onion powder

paprika

chili powder

gluten-free corn taco shells

1 can of corn, cooked

cornstarch

cumin

1 can refried beans, cooked

½ cup chopped onion

olive oil

salt and pepper

1/3 cup mild salsa

1 can of gluten-free beef broth, plus water

1 Mix together in a small bowl and set aside:

1 tsp onion power
1 tsp chili power
½ tsp cumin
1 tsp each salt and pepper
½ tsp celery seed
½ tsp paprika
2 tbsp cornstarch

2 Cook rice according to directions on package, but substitute ½ can of broth for ½ cup of the water.

3 Brown ground beef until fully cooked.

4 Add the other ½ can of broth to meat.

5 Add the spice and cornstarch mixture to meat.

6 Stir on medium heat until meat sauce thickens, adding water if needed.

7 Set meat mixture on low and cover.

8 Sauté onion and bell peppers with 1 tsp olive oil for 3 to 4 minutes.

9 Add onion and peppers to cooked corn and toss.

10 Add salsa to cooked rice and toss.

Serve tacos with the CORN, BEANS, and RICE on the side. Use condiments of your choice, and ENJOY!